VIRGINIA UNDER CHARLES I AND CROMWELL, 1625-1660

By

Wilcomb E. Washburn
Research Associate, Institute
of Early American History and Culture

and

Instructor in History,
College of William and Mary

Virginia 350th Anniversary Celebration Corporation
Williamsburg, Virginia

1957

975.5
ℒw 4

36371
April 1958

Jamestown 350th Anniversary
Historical Booklet, Number 7

Virginia Under Charles I and Cromwell, 1625-1660

VIRGINIA ON THE EVE OF EXPANSION

Woodrow Wilson named the first volume of his *History of the United States* "The Swarming of the English." We might go further and compare the colonization and expansion in the New World to a fissioning process in which individual atoms are torn loose from a former pattern of coherence and fused into new and strange patterns. The United States, indeed, is still in the process of fusion following the earlier fission process. It has not yet reached the stability that comes to some nations in history, and which is marked by a fixed pattern of population growth, land use, day-to-day habits, and philosophic beliefs. It is, rather, a country in which every generation can look back to a strangely different era that existed before it came of age.

The period 1625-1660 in Virginia history is an important one for the study of the fission-fusion process in America. During those years Virginia's population increased perhaps twenty-five or thirty fold, and the settlements spread from a thin belt along the James River to the whole of Tidewater Virginia. Human atoms were propelled outwards in every direction in an uncontrolled and only feebly directed expansion.

The years 1607 to 1625 had created a base for this expansion. Those had been crucial years and difficult ones. Settlements had resembled military camps and individual colonists had been commanded like soldiers. Rigorous administration of justice, fear of the Indians, and the strict economic regulations imposed by the London Company had served to restrain the potentially expansive nature of the colonists.

The year 1625 saw Virginia under a new King and under a new form of government. The charter of the London Company

1

was made void, and the colony passed from the control of a commercial company to the direct control of King Charles I.

The official census of the non-Indian population of Virginia in 1625 showed 1,232 persons in the colony. Nine hundred and fifty-two were males, twelve of them Negroes. Two hundred and eighty were females, eleven of them Negroes. Although the colony had been in existence for eighteen years the fissioning process had hardly begun. But it was beginning. Five years later the population had more than doubled to approximately 3,000. In 1640 the population jumped to 8,000, and by 1670 to 40,000, of whom 2,000 were Negroes. Every aspect of Virginia life—political, physical, economic, social, and moral—was to be affected by this explosive and uncontrolled growth.

Virginia did not develop any cities or even towns during the period 1625-1660. Indeed, the towns, such as Jamestown and Henrico, that had earlier been established, declined in population or were totally abandoned. The immigrants who were funneled into the colony through Jamestown were soon attracted to the ever widening frontier. During the first twenty years colonists had lived in organized farming communities, separated from other such settlements, but strictly supervised by local "plantation commanders." The separate settlements were variously called "colonies," "plantations," "hundreds," and "particular plantations," and sometimes contained hundreds of planters. Frequently the "plantation'" was located within a loop of the James River. The members of the settlement planted their crops within the loop, and set up palisades and forts at the open end for their common defense. Sentinels and guards were provided cooperatively to man the defenses. As the settlers increased in numbers and the power of their governors and of the Indians to restrain them decreased, however, they tended to leave the organized communities and to carve out for themselves individual plantations in the wilderness. Thus, even while the population of the colony grew by leaps and bounds, the population of Jamestown and other areas where population was once concentrated declined. It was a process, one might call it, of de-urbanization.

What was it that reversed the process of urbanization that was going on in the mother country? The attraction was, of course, the land and its fruits. England, with her five or six millions, was not overpopulated by modern standards. Nor was she overpopulated by comparison with the great nations of the Orient such as China which could even in that period count its population in the hundreds of millions. But her few millions seemed at times to oppress the English soil. On the other hand, America was a relatively new home of the human species. Perhaps less than a million Indians lived within the present bounds of the United States, and the Indians with whom the English in Virginia came in contact numbered less than 10,000. "In the beginning all the world was America," wrote John Locke, and the English townsmen, villagers, and yeomen who came to America found it natural to revert back to the time when Adam went forth from the Garden of Eden to till the ground from whence he was taken. It would be more truthful to say, however, that the English went not so much in sorrow as in confidence, as the sons of Abraham to whom God had promised all the land of Canaan for an everlasting possession.

Tobacco was the richest fruit of the land. Despite the moral opprobrium in which the "vile, stinking weed" was held by men in England, including King James himself, the public soon developed an insatiable appetite for it. Having for the Europeans the attraction of novelty and utility, it commanded an enormous price in the early years of the settlement. With Spanish tobacco selling at eighteen shillings a pound in 1619, the opportunities for gain from tobacco production seemed unlimited. Here was the "gold" that Virginia had to offer, and soon all hands could think of nothing else. The earliest settlers, hoping to emulate the Spaniards in finding great treasures and living off the labor of the Indians, had suffered bitterly from shortages of food. Later

3

settlers, though they did not hold to the expectations of the first arrivals, still sought the avenue of quickest and greatest gain, and tobacco provided that avenue. Throughout the 1620's many planters neglected to grow corn or wheat, preferring to obtain their food supply by barter or seizure from the Indians, or by purchase from planters who were willing to divert their labor to such crops. Who would bother with grain when tobacco sold for as much per pound as grain did per bushel? Frenchmen, brought over to introduce vine-growing in the colony, neglected their specialty to plant tobacco and had to be restrained by an act of February 1632. An act of February 1633 similarly required all gunsmiths, brickmakers, carpenters, joiners, sawyers, and turners to work at their trades and not to plant tobacco or do other work in the ground.

Another booklet in this series deals with agriculture in Virginia. It is enough to say here that as the total production of tobacco increased so did the price decline. Our present-day farm surplus problem is not new. Even when the price had plummeted to a penny a pound the planters were not discouraged from planting. Attempts were made on both sides of the Atlantic to fix prices and to control the amount of production in order to restore prosperity to the tobacco farmers. The important questions were whose interests would be served, and how would they be served best?

The death of James I and the dissolution of the Virginia Company occurred almost at the same time. Charles I, his son, assumed the throne in 1625 and promptly assured the planters that though the form of Virginia's government had changed, the individual planters could be sure that their rights and property would be respected. Charles informed the colonists, however, that he would take over the buying of their tobacco as a royal monopoly and give them such prices as would satisfy and encourage them. Agreement with the planters, nevertheless, was difficult to obtain. The Virginians were solidly united as a special interest in favoring the highest prices and the greatest pro-

4

duction. Their representatives, both in the House of Burgesses and on the Council, were their ardent spokesmen, themselves planters, whose interest lay in fighting the battle of all Virginians. On the other hand the King, and the English merchants and associates through whom he dealt, desired to buy Virginia's tobacco at the lowest possible prices and in moderate quantities. The tug of war between the two sides continued for many years without any clear-cut resolution.

Virginia under Wyatt and Yeardley, 1625-1627: Tobacco and Defense

Sir Francis Wyatt, who had been the London Company's Governor in the period 1621-1624, was appointed Governor by James I the first year the colony was under royal control. Although the King made no specific provision for the continuation of a representative Assembly, Wyatt and the Council called together representatives of the various settlements to meet in a General Assembly on May 10, 1625, in Jamestown. There they drew up a petition complaining of the old Company rule and the miserable state in which it had kept the colony during the previous twelve years, and pleading with the King not to allow a monopoly of the tobacco trade. The King's advisers, they feared, were those who had formerly oppressed them and who would do so again should the King consent to a "pernitious contract" taking all their tobacco at unfair rates. To present their case against the contract they chose Sir George Yeardley, former Governor, to go to England as their agent. The willingness of Wyatt and the Council to call such an Assembly and the unanimity of views deriving from it, show how single in their economic interests all Virginians were.

Governor Wyatt attempted to prevent disorderly expansion of settlement and to build positions of strength in the colony, but he knew that the "affection" of the planters to "their privat dividents" was too strong a force to resist. Hence he recommended that a palisade be built from Martin's Hundred on the James River to

Chiskiack on the York River, with houses spaced along it at convenient intervals. In this way the Indians might be kept out of the entire lower portion of the peninsula, the cattle kept in, and the colony provided with a secure base for the development of its economy. After the economy was flourishing, there would be a chance for finding the riches in the mountains to the west and the longed-for passage to the South Sea, so confidently believed to lie just beyond the Appalachians. All these enterprises presupposed the "winning of the Forest" between the York and the James, which Wyatt hoped to accomplish by means of his palisade scheme.

Wyatt's project was not immediately put into effect. In 1626 he was replaced by Sir George Yeardley. Yeardley, like Wyatt, devoted much of his time to devising means to promote the security of the colony against attack by land or by sea.

It is hard for us to realize how desperately concerned with their security were the few thousand Englishmen who inhabited Virginia at this time. Separated from the mother country by 3,000 miles of ocean, a dangerous crossing usually taking two months, the settlers had only a precarious toe hold on a vast continent. From the ocean side the settlers feared possible attack from other European colonizing powers: the Spanish, French, or Dutch. The Spanish ambassador in London in the early period of the Virginia settlement had frequently urged his government to wipe out the struggling colony. But the indecision of Spain's monarch had saved the colony.

The Virginians themselves had engaged in expeditions against the French settled in Maine, and spoke menacingly of the Dutch who had established a settlement on the King's domain in Hudson's River in 1613. The claims of the European monarchs to the American continent conflicted with one another, and there seemed little chance that a resolution would come by any other means than war. So it proved to be, later. In the meantime, at home, Virginia settlers stood on guard. Governor Yeardley appointed

6

Capt. William Tucker, one of the Virginia Council, to check at Point Comfort all ships entering the James River. Tucker was provided with a well-armed shallop and absolute authority to check all ships arriving. He could not do battle with an enemy warship, of course, but he could give the alarm in case the enemy appeared. A few years later a fort was built at Point Comfort to defend the entrance to Virginia's great river. Although the channel was too wide ever to be adequately commanded by the cannon of the day, the fort provided some protection to the colony.

Yeardley made similar efforts to strengthen Virginia's position on land against the numerically superior Indians. Like Wyatt he urged the necessity of "planting the forest" rather than jumping beyond it to areas far from existing settlements. As a means of controlling the population Yeardley issued a proclamation requiring that anyone who desired to move his place of residence within the colony must obtain prior permission from the Governor and Council. Even to be absent for a short time from his place of residence, a planter was required to get permission from his "plantation commander." As was pointed out earlier, "plantations" in this early period were usually not the individually-owned, individually-operated plantations of later times, but "private colonies" or "particular plantations," organized on a joint-stock basis, on which more than a hundred men might live.

In keeping with his conception of the colony as a military outpost, Yeardley made plans for an armed settlement on the York at Chiskiack, and devised a project for a surprise attack on all the surrounding Indians on the first day of August 1627. Each "particular plantation" was to march against an Indian town, kill as many Indians as possible, and seize or cut down what corn it could. The attack was a success, but because of a scarcity of shot the English failed in their desired goal of utterly extirpating the red men.

In November 1627 Yeardley died, and the Council chose one

of its number, Captain Francis West, to assume the role of Governor and Captain General.

Virginia under Francis West and Dr. John Pott, 1627-1630

Meanwhile the King had grown increasingly disgusted that Virginia's economy continued to be "built on smoke," and he ordered the Virginians to concentrate on crops and products other than tobacco. Among the products urged on the colonists were iron, salt, pitch and tar, potash, and pipe staves. As his directives went unheeded, the King determined to force a drastic reduction in the planting of the profitable tobacco crop. In instructions sent out in 1627 he directed that no master of a family be allowed to plant above 200 pounds of tobacco and no servant more than 125 pounds. He also ordered that all tobacco was to be consigned to him or his representatives.

Charles directed that a general assembly of the planters' representatives be summoned to deal with his proposals, and Governor West and the Council ordered an Assembly to meet on March 10, 1628. The Assembly thanked the King for prohibiting the importation of Spanish tobacco into the English market, but cried that they would be at the mercy of covetous individuals in England if a monopoly on Virginia tobacco was allowed. They proposed, however, that since the King intended to take all their tobacco, he should agree to take at least 500,000 pounds of tobacco at 3 shillings 6 pence the pound delivered in Virginia, or 4 shillings delivered in London. If the King was unwilling to take so much, they desired the right to export again from England to the Low Countries, Ireland, Turkey, and elsewhere. As to the King's proposal to limit tobacco cultivation to 200 pounds for the master of a family and 125 pounds for a servant, "every weake judgment," they asserted, could see that this would not be sufficient for their maintenance. As to the King's desire that the colonists should produce pitch and tar, pipe staves, and iron, they complained that much capital was needed to put such

8

KING CHARLES I
Painting by Daniel Mytens

enterprises in operation. Few planters either could or would undertake such schemes when tobacco culture required so little capital and produced such quick and profitable results.

The Assembly commissioned Sir Francis Wyatt, then in England, and two Virginians to represent them in negotiations with the King. They were to be allowed to come down six pence on each of the figures insisted upon by Governor, Council, and Burgesses in their answer to the King's letter.

As in 1625, the opportunity to join in Assembly for the purpose of agreeing on regulations for tobacco production allowed the planters to deal with other matters. Wesley Frank Craven has written that "representative government in America owes much in its origins to an attempt to win men's support of a common economic program by means of mutual consent." Had the King been less desirous of taking every planter's tobacco and less concerned with the neglect of staple commodities, he might well have governed the colony without calling the planters together in periodic "assemblies."

Dr. John Pott was elected by the Council on March 5, 1629, to succeed West as Governor, and he governed in Virginia for one year. Few men possess a less savory record than this first representative of the medical profession in America. In 1624 he had been ordered removed from the Virginia Council, at the insistence of the Earl of Warwick, for his part in the attempt to poison the colony's Indian foes. He was later convicted of cattle stealing but spared punishment because he was the only doctor in the colony and therefore in great demand.

Both West and Pott were foes of the Indians, and in numerous orders and proclamations denounced former treaties of peace with them, and directed that perpetual enmity and wars be maintained against them. A pretended peace was, however, authorized to be extended to the Indians in August 1628 until certain captive Englishmen were redeemed; then it was to be broken.

The colonists, too, suffered during the administrations of West and Pott. One man expressed the hope for "an Easterly wind to blow to send in Noble Capt. Harvey, And then I shall have wright for all my wrong." Capt. John Harvey was known in the colony for the investigation he had conducted in Virginia in 1624-1625, and the King had appointed him Governor on March 26, 1628. Harvey did not actually take up his government in Virginia until two years later. In the meantime West and Pott administered the colony.

Virginia under John Harvey, 1630-1632: Expansion and Development

When Harvey arrived in 1630 he found that inadequate restrictions placed on tobacco production in the previous years had created an enormous surplus which had forced the price down to a penny a pound. Harvey found also that because of their "greedie desires to make store of Tobackoe," the settlers had neglected to plant sufficient corn, let alone to develop different commodities as instructed by the King. Calling an Assembly, he convinced the representatives to agree to reduce the amount of tobacco planted, and to increase the amount of corn. He also sent ships into the Chesapeake and southward to Cape Fear to trade for corn with the Indians to make up the deficit left by the negligent planters. But most important of all, Harvey put into effect the long-dreamed-of plan to secure the entire area between the James and the York by building a palisade between Archer's Hope Creek (now College Creek), emptying into the James River, and Queen's Creek, emptying into the York River. Harvey's plan called also for a settlement on the south side of the York. This outpost would serve as an advance base and point of defense for operations against Opechancanough, King of the Pamunkeys, and his many warriors. Six hundred acres apiece were granted there in 1630 to Capt. John West, brother of Lord Delaware, and to Capt. John Utie, who were made commanders of the settlement. Fifty acres were offered to any person who would settle there during the first year of its existence and twenty-five during

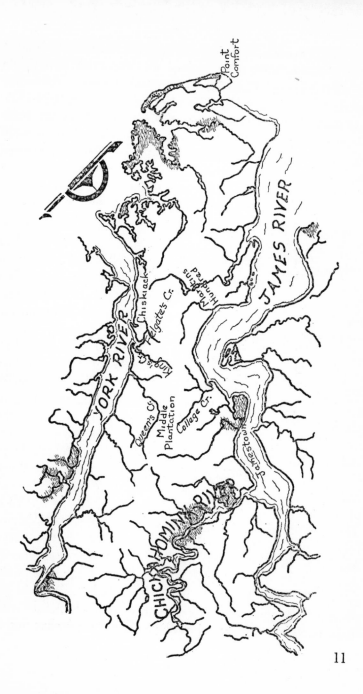

the next year. Exactly when the first settlers moved to the York is uncertain, but it was probably in 1631. West and Utie settled on either side of a bay formed by the joining of King's Creek and Felgate's Creek about four miles above modern Yorktown. The tourist who speeds along the Colonial Parkway from Jamestown to Yorktown crosses the bay within sight of the tracts granted West and Utie. Today he may drive from Jamestown to the York with comfort and safety in a few minutes. It took the early settlers twenty-four years to cover the same distance.

About the same time, probably in 1630, another distant settlement was established. William Claiborne, Secretary of the Council of State of Virginia, with one hundred men, settled Kent Island 150 miles up Chesapeake Bay. In the Assembly of February 1632 both "Kiskyacke and the Isle of Kent" were represented by Capt. Nicholas Martiau, ancestor of George Washington.

The great expansion had now begun. Settlers crossed from the James to the York, and provision was made by an act of the Assembly of February 1633 for building houses at Middle Plantation, situated strategically between College Creek and Queen's Creek, and for "securing" the tract of land lying between the two creeks.

Besides being concerned with questions of defense, Harvey pursued a policy of encouraging trade with other colonies in the New World. Numerous commissions were issued by the Governor in March and April of 1632 authorizing individuals to trade with New England, Nova Scotia, and the Dutch plantation in Hudson's River, as well as with the West Indies. Harvey even gave instructions to Nathaniel Basse, one of the traders and a member of the Council, to encourage people from the other colonies to come to Virginia. "If those of Newe England shall dislike the coldnes of there clymate or the barrenness of the soyle," wrote Harvey, "you may propose unto them the plantinge of Delaware bay, where they shall have what furtherance wee cann afford them, and noe impediment objected against theire owne orders and lawes."

But all was not well in the government of the colony. Harvey found the Council members constantly opposing him, disputing his authority, resisting his attempts to administer equal justice to all men. The royal Governor was not supreme as we now sometimes mistakenly assume. He was first among equals only. Decisions at this time were made by majority vote, and the Governor was frequently outvoted. Moreover the Councilors, who could devote more of their time to their private affairs, tended to be better off financially than the Governor himself, who found it next to impossible to get his salary from the King, and who was forced to entertain at his own expense all who came to James City. Harvey complained that he should be called the "host" rather than the "Governor" of Virginia. In contrast, Samuel Mathews, one of Harvey's enemies on the Council, owned the finest estate in Virginia. William Claiborne, another of Harvey's enemies on the Council, besides a large estate, had a royal commission and English backers for his powerful trading company.

Harvey made every effort to reconcile the differences which arose between him and the Council members, and on December 20, 1631, all signed an agreement promising to work in harmony and to mend their discontent.

Fortified by this agreement, Harvey went forward with his efforts to put Virginia's agricultural economy on a sound basis. The principal problem was to force the planters to diversify. Many tears are shed for the poverty of the planters of Virginia, and their customary indebtedness to English creditors is usually cited as proof of their poverty. But this "poverty" was not based on the inability of the planter to raise enough food to support himself and his family, but on the fluctuations of the market price of the crop—tobacco—to which he had devoted most of his energies as a speculative venture. Strange as it may seem, the planter had to be forced to raise enough food for his own support, so avid was his desire for quick tobacco profits.

Governor Harvey's Assembly of February 1632 directed that every man working in the ground should plant and tend at least two acres of corn per head, on penalty of forfeiture of his entire crop of tobacco. Harvey hoped to make Virginia "the granarie to his Majesty's Empire," as Sicily had been to Rome. Another act allowed corn to be sold for as high a price as could be obtained, contrary to the usual European and colonial habit of fixing prices on basic commodities used by the people. The reason given for this freedom from price fixing was that the precedents of other countries did not apply to America, "for none are so poore heere, as that they may not have as much corne, as they will plant, havinge land enough."

The Assembly of 1632 did, however, fix a price on tobacco, requiring that it not be sold at less than six pence per pound, a law they went to great pains to justify to the King. Tobacco was Virginia's primary economic interest, and the Virginians were willing to go to any lengths to advance that interest. They urged the King not to place any impediment to their "free trade," or right to sell their tobacco wherever they could, and mentioned that they had already constructed several barques and had begun trading with the Dutch plantation on Hudson's River. Governor Harvey asked why the English merchants could not afford to allow them a penny a pound for their tobacco when the Dutch paid eighteen pence per pound.

The English merchants who traded with Virginia formed a tight little group which used its favored position to charge excessive prices for English-made goods, and to give abnormally low prices for Virginia tobacco. Such a policy was not entirely owing to covetousness. The English economy was shackled by a conception of economic life which believed in the necessity of monopolies and restrictive devices of all sorts. The Dutch nation, on the other hand, had thrown off many of the traditional mercantilist restraints on trade. Holland soon enjoyed a level of prosperity that made her the envy of the rest of Europe. Her rivals attributed Dutch success to the energy of her people. "Go to beat the Dutch" became a byword which has persisted to this day. Not until a century later did the English realize that Dutch prosperity was caused not so much by hard work as by the policy of freeing trade from unnecessary restraints. As Dutch prosperity increased, Dutch ships appeared in every sea, underselling all rivals and paying better prices for local products. The complaint that the London merchants allowed only one penny a pound for the Virginians' tobacco while the Dutch gave eighteen strikingly illustrates the measure of Dutch commercial superiority. No wonder that the London merchants should demand that the Dutch be excluded from the Virginia market! For the same reason Virginians, whether Governors, Councilors, Burgesses, or planters, were, throughout the seventeenth century, almost unanimously opposed to the English government's policy of restricting trade with Virginia to English ships and confining that trade to English ports.

Although Governor Harvey supported the Burgesses and Council in their strong defense of tobacco production, he privately wrote that he had not only endeavored to have reduced the amount of tobacco planted "but if it might have been, to have utterly rooted out this stinking commodity." He reported that only the powerful hand of the King and his Council could, however, effect such an end, so "indeared" were the planters to the traffic. Moreover, Harvey admitted that until some more staple commodity could be developed, tobacco could not be prohibited without the utter ruin of the colony. Virginia was rooted to tobacco—seemingly for ever.

The Virginia planters' proposals, of course, met the opposition of the London merchants, who complained to their powerful friends and associates in the government and urged the King and his Council to nullify the restrictions which the Virginians tried to place on the sale of their tobacco. The merchants were particularly opposed to the desire of the Virginians to by-pass them and trade with foreign nations directly.

It is hard for us to realize today the immense importance of merchants and traders in influencing the colonial policies of the English government. Virginia was founded by a commercial company. All the early attempts at settlement were made by private persons who were willing to "adventure" their capital or their skill. Behind the great explorers stood private individuals who risked their money on the success of the voyage or settlement. The "government"—perhaps it would be truer to say the Kings and their advisers—did not have the funds or the foresight to support these ventures. They were perfectly willing to sign papers granting lands they did not own to those who were willing to attempt the settlement, but they were reluctant to put up their own money except on a sure thing.

Once the settlements were functioning, once revenues were patently obvious, the monarchs showed more concern with their government. Merchants still, however, continued to provide the link between the King and colony to a great extent. In an age of state regulation and monopolies, in an age which did not provide fixed salaries for men in high position, there was a close relationship between the Exchange and the Court. A merchant dealing with overseas trade could not be successful unless he had influence at Court. Even after the King took away the charter of the Virginia Company, merchants continued to apply pressure to the committees and commissions set up to advise the King on colonial policy. Although the colonists feared that Charles I might reinstitute a company over them, and the former representatives of the Virginia Company pressed for such a move, the merchants were not able to re-establish direct control over the colony.

16

Virginia Under Harvey, 1632-1634: Prosperity and Decentralization

In September 1632, under Governor Harvey's direction, the first revisal of Virginia's laws was made. Twenty-five years of experience under varying forms of government lay behind the revisal. All previous laws were examined and brought into conformity with existing conditions. Most of the legislation concerned the Church, tobacco, and the Indians, good indications of what most concerned the early settlers. Highways were also authorized to be laid out in convenient places, the first sign that settlement was spreading from the rivers—the traditional highways of Virginia—into the interior. Virginia was becoming more than a military outpost. It was becoming a "home."

The success of Harvey's attempt to stabilize and diversify agricultural production is confirmed in the account of Captain Thomas Young of his voyage to Virginia and Delaware Bay in 1634. Sailing up the James River he noticed that "the cuntry aboundeth with very great plentie of milk, cheese, butter and corne, which latter almost every planter in the country hath." The grim threat of starvation that had in former times hung over the colony had been dispelled. Although there had been a rapid increase in population, the food supply more than kept up with the increase, and thousands of bushels of corn were even transported and sold to the New England colonists.

The year 1634 also marked the establishment of the county form of local government in Virginia. The scattered plantations and settlements, rapidly expanding and hence more difficult to govern from James City, were now organized into eight counties. For each a monthly court was established by commission from the Governor and Council. Provision for separate courts in outlying areas had been made as early as 1618. Now the shift to decentralized government was formalized.

Northampton C.

Charles James R.

Appomatox R.

City C.

York C.

York R.

Warwick C.

Surry C.

Elizabeth City C.

James R.

Isle of Wight C.

Nansemond C.

Lower Norfolk C.

Chowan R.

Roanoke R.

THE "THRUSTING OUT" OF GOVERNOR HARVEY AND ITS AFTERMATH, 1635-1641

In 1635, in one of the most famous incidents in Virginia's early history, Governor Harvey was deposed by his Council. Many historians have assumed that Harvey was deposed by a spontaneous uprising of the people no longer able to bear his oppressive government. There is, however, little justification for this view. Many more accusations have been hurled at Harvey by later historians than by his contemporaries, and it is undoubtedly Harvey's position as a royal Governor and his quick temper that have caused historians to take such a hostile view of him. Ever since the successful American Revolution of 1776, American historians, in interpreting the events of the colonial period, have jumped at any evidence of discontent as an anticipation of, and justification for, the War for Independence. They have not stopped to determine whether the charges hurled at the royal Governors were true or not. It is enough that someone accused them of oppression.

The causes of the revolt against Harvey were various. Of first importance was the continual opposition that existed between the Governor and his Council. The revolt was not primarily a revolt of the people but a revolt by certain members of the Council who attempted to give their particular insubordination the appearance of a general rebellion.

Harvey's commission was such that he could do nothing except by majority vote of himself and the Council sitting as a single body. The Council frequently outvoted him, effectively blocking his proposals. Harvey bitterly disputed the Council's power to thwart his will. He pointed out that the King had sent him to Virginia not only as the new Governor but with the specific duty of correcting the abuses that were reported to have existed under previous Governors, especially those abuses for which members of the Council were responsible. Previous to his arrival the government had been in the hands of Francis

West and Dr. John Pott, elected to office by the other members of the Council. Pott, whose reputation has been mentioned earlier, was not pleased to be brought to justice for his dishonest actions. Nor was Samuel Mathews, an important member of the Council, pleased to be brought to justice for withholding the cattle and property of other men. (Mathews, the richest man in the colony, successfully resisted all legal attempts to divest him of this property.) Nor were the Council members pleased when, in accordance with His Majesty's commands, Harvey attempted to punish those responsible for the ill treatment of William Capps, sent earlier by the King to start production of tar, potash, salt, pipe staves and other commodities. The Council had discouraged him from his mission, except in so far as it concerned the production of salt, and Pott had issued an order preventing him from leaving the colony to report to the King.

Another cause for grievance against Harvey was the peace he made with the local Indians. The colonists distrusted the Indians more than they distrusted other Europeans. The great massacre of 1622, when the Indians made a desperate attempt to destroy the English settlement, had placed Indian-white relations on a basis of perpetual enmity. Legally, the Indians had never been considered to have the same rights as the English. English law throughout the seventeenth century maintained the doctrine that between Christians and infidels there could exist nothing but perpetual enmity, a view which was a hangover from the period of the Crusades, wars against the Turks, and expansion by militant Christian nations into heathen lands during the fifteenth and sixteenth centuries. It is true that practical co-operation and on-the-spot recognition of Indian rights had developed in Virginia in the early years. The massacre of 1622, however, gave Virginians an excuse for abandoning all forms of co-operation with, and respect for, the Indians. Deceit and breach of faith were elevated into acknowledged instruments of policy. The right of the Indians even to occupy the land of their forefathers was denied. They were admitted to exist and to hold land *in fact,* but the English refused to recognize *in law* either their existence or their title to land. Total extirpation was resolved against those Indian nations which had taken part in the massacre. "Marches" were periodically ordered against the various tribes with the purpose of destroying or seizing their corn, burning their shelters, and killing as many members of the tribe as possible.

Governor Harvey reversed this policy and made peace with the Indians against the advice of Dr. Pott and other Councilors. He also attempted to see that some measure of equity was extended to Indian-white relations. As a result, the more aggressive planters accused him of promoting a second massacre.

What really set off the revolt against Harvey, however, was the injection of the hottest issue of the day into the controversy: whether Harvey was "soft" on Catholicism. This issue was brought to a head because of the grant of a portion of Virginia's original territory to George Calvert, first Lord Baltimore. Harvey had extended a helping hand to Baltimore's colonists. Although his actions in this regard were specifically required of him by the King, and although he received especially warm commendation from the English government for doing so, the Virginia colonists objected. The King's grant, for one thing, had been carved out of the Virginia Company's old bounds which had been left undisturbed when the Company lost its right to govern the area. Already Virginians were beginning to eye the benefits of settlement in the northern reaches of Chesapeake Bay. One, Colonel William Claiborne, Secretary of the colony, had obtained a royal commission to trade in the area and had established a settlement on Kent Island, opposite the present Annapolis, far up Chesapeake Bay. By acting on the King's instructions and supporting Baltimore's authority in the area against Claiborne's claims, Harvey turned the second most important man in the colony against him.

Harvey at first backed the Virginia Council's assertion that

Kent Island was a part of Virginia, and not part of the supposedly uncultivated wilderness granted to Baltimore by the King. But in the face of Charles's obvious desire to take the area away from Virginia, and because Claiborne's patent authorized trade rather than settlement, Harvey soon accepted Lord Baltimore's position that Claiborne's trading post lay within the limits of Baltimore's jurisdiction. Irritation between the two men increased when Harvey attempted jointly with the Maryland authorities to conduct an examination of charges that Claiborne was stirring up Maryland's Indians against the new settlers. Claiborne was accused of telling the local Indians that the new settlers were not Englishmen but Spaniards. The investigation which ensued was hampered at every turn by Claiborne and his friends on the Virginia Council.

The Virginians were most concerned not by the apparent violation of Virginia's territorial integrity, but by the fact that the new settlement was being established and settled by Roman Catholics. The Virginians were less tolerant than the King in wishing success to Lord Baltimore, a Catholic, and his fellow religionists, in establishing a colony on their northern border. The Virginia Council wrote Charles in 1629 thanking him for "the freedome of our Religion which wee have enjoyed," and asserting proudly that "noe papists have beene suffered to settle amongst us." They insisted upon tendering the oaths of supremacy and allegiance to Lord Baltimore when he arrived in Virginia in October 1629 to consider a possible settlement, and reported to the King that he had refused to take those oaths. Charles I had married a Catholic, Henrietta Maria of France, and, like his father, James I, was not disposed to allow too rigorous penalties against those who professed religious allegiance to Rome. But the Parliament, and the people in general, feared and hated Catholics, believing their religious beliefs to be incompatible with loyalty to a Protestant state.

By means of the oaths of allegiance and supremacy Catholics

were required to recognize the English sovereign as their right-ful ruler in matters spiritual and ecclesiastical as well as temporal, to repudiate the papal claim to depose heretical princes, to promise to fight for the King in case of rebellion caused by a papal sentence of deposition, and to denounce the doctrine that princes, being excommunicated, could be deposed or murdered, or that subjects could be absolved from their oath of allegiance. The oaths were based on a real fear which identified Roman Catholicism with treason. Protestants felt that Catholics owed their highest allegiance to a foreign power, and hence were not good Englishmen. The problem was a complicated one, and much debated at the time and since. Now it is generally accepted that one can owe spiritual allegiance to Rome while remaining a faithful subject of a non-Catholic state. In England in the seventeenth century, however, the Church of Rome was too closely identified with England's mortal enemies to allow her freely to tolerate Catholics in her midst. For a long period England had feared Spain as the greatest threat to her existence. Even after the defeat of the Spanish Armada in 1588 this fear persisted and to a certain extent was transferred to France, another Catholic power. The measures taken against the Catholics in England were similar to those taken against Communists in this country today, and they were taken for the same reason: the fear that the followers of a universal ideology would turn against their local allegiance if the two ever came in conflict.

Eventually Charles's easy attitude towards Catholics helped bring about his downfall. In a similar way Harvey's compliance with the King's instructions to aid and respect Baltimore's colonists weakened his popularity in Virginia.

As the locus of power in England shifted from the King and his lords towards the Parliament and the people, a stronger Protestant and democratic policy became necessary. The eventual result of this shift in power became evident with the beheading of Charles I in 1649 and, later, with the Glorious Revolution of

1689 and the crowning of William and Mary as constitutional symbols of the power of the English nation.

So great was the popular feeling in Virginia against the "Papists" in Maryland that many, in casual conversation, exclaimed that they would rather knock their cattle on the head than sell them to Maryland. To accommodate the needs of the new settlers in Maryland, Harvey sent them some cows of his own and did his best to ease their early struggles, in accordance with the King's commands. He could not do all he wished, however, because he was frequently outvoted at the Council meetings on anything that had to do with Maryland.

The deposition of Governor Harvey had its origin on April 27, 1635, in a mutinous gathering held in the York River area, Virginia's first frontier settlement outside the James River. The ringleader seems to have been Francis Pott, brother of Doctor Pott, who harangued the meeting about the alleged injustice of Governor Harvey, and about the Governor's toleration for Indians, which he said would bring on another massacre. Francis Pott had formerly been commander of the fort at Point Comfort but had a short time before been discharged by Harvey for misbehavior.

Harvey ordered the principals in the York meeting arrested, and called the Council together to consider what action should be taken against them. The Council opposed Harvey's desire to proceed against them by martial law, and began to excuse the dissidents on the grounds of the many complaints the people had about the government. Harvey thereupon demanded opinions in writing on what should be done with the mutineers. George Menefie, the first Councilor of whom Harvey demanded such a written statement, said he was but a young lawyer and dared not give a sudden opinion. A violent debate ensued. The rest of the Council also refused to put their opinions in writing. At the next meeting of the Council, Menefie began to recount the grievances of the country, naming Harvey's detention of the Assembly's letter to the King as the principal one. The original of this letter, refusing the King's propositions concerning a tobacco contract, Harvey had retained, as likely to infuriate the monarch and do the country no good. Instead he had sent a copy of the letter to the Secretary of State. At Menefie's words, Harvey, in a rage, brought his hand down sharply on the Councilor's shoulder and said, "Do you say so? I arrest you on suspicion of treason to his Majesty." Then Capt. John Utie and Capt. Samuel Mathews seized Harvey and said, "And we you upon suspicion of treason to his Majesty." Secretary Richard Kemp immediately stepped between the men and told Utie and Mathews that Harvey was the King's Lieutenant and that they had done more than they could answer for. Mathews and Utie released their hold on the Governor but demanded that he go to England to answer the people's complaints. To emphasize their demand Dr. John Pott signaled forty soldiers who had been concealed outside the Governor's house (where the meeting was held) to march up to the door, apparently as a form of threat, although the mutineers protested that the guard was for the Governor's safety. More days of negotiations passed. The rebellious Council called an Assembly to hear charges against Harvey, and chose Capt. John West to be Governor until His Majesty's pleasure might be known. Finally Harvey agreed to return to England. Francis Pott went on the same ship home.

In England the Privy Council heard the charges against Harvey and his defense. None of the accusations stood up, and he was able to show why the Council had private reasons to desire his removal. The King directed him to return to his government with increased power, and ordered the Councilors who had been instrumental in deposing him to be sent to England for trial. Harvey was able to collect some of his back pay and to obtain the King's agreement that he should return in a ship of war. Unfortunately, an old and unseaworthy prize ship was provided him which had to turn back shortly after its departure, and Harvey was forced to take passage on an ordinary merchant ship which arrived in Virginia January 18, 1637. Harvey suffered great losses because of the unseaworthiness of the prize ship, and petitioned the King for recompense. He was, however, ordered to pay out of his own pocket all the losses he had sustained by the affair, although he was authorized to collect an equivalent amount from the estates of the mutinous Councilors should they be convicted.

The sending of the mutinous Councilors—Capt. John West, Samuel Mathews, John Utie, and William Pierce—as prisoners to England, strangely enough allowed them to accomplish what they had been unable to do in Virginia. So many and so powerful were their friends, so wealthy were they themselves, and so many were the charges that they contrived against Harvey now that he was back in the colony and unable to answer them, that the King soon reversed himself and ordered Harvey relieved of his post. The King's action illustrates one of the little appreciated factors in American colonial history: the role played by petitions to the King. Three thousand miles of ocean, and months, even years, in time, separated the assertion from the proof, encouraged the most exaggerated charges, and contributed to the unjustified sympathy extended by the King to many petitioners who did not deserve such consideration. Some of the "crimes" charged against Harvey were even discovered to have their origin in the King's own commands or in earlier acts of Assembly. Yet they contributed to clouding the atmosphere and blinding the lords of England to the true worth of their representative in Virginia.

On the basis of unjustified or unsupported charges concerning Harvey's alleged misappropriation of the mutinous Councilors' estates, which had been seized for the King pending their trial, the King, on May 25, 1637, ordered these estates returned to their owners. Harvey complied immediately as far as four of the Councilors were concerned, but he had already allowed legal action to be directed against Mathews' estate by those who had claims against Mathews, and judgments had been made in favor of the plaintiffs. When the English government heard he had not turned back Mathews' property, it promptly ordered that he do so without delay, which order Harvey then tried to put into effect as best he could. The damage had been done, however, and the impression created that he had willfully misappropriated Mathews' property and disobeyed the King's commands.

Harvey's fight against the charges his enemies brought against him in England suffered another blow when Mr. Anthony Panton, a minister who had been twice banished from the colony, returned to England to add his complaints to those of the others. Harvey was not given a chance to defend himself against the new charges, and on January 11, 1639, Sir Francis Wyatt was appointed to succeed him.

On Wyatt's arrival Harvey's estate was seized and the old Governor prevented from returning to England until he could satisfy his creditors. To meet their demands, Harvey, in 1640, was forced to sell all his land and much of his personal property. The fact that he was in debt to many persons in the colony is itself a significant indication that he had not abused the powers of his office. It is a curious fact that both Governor Sir William Berkeley and Governor Harvey were much in debt when the rebellions against their rule began, while their principal enemies were among the wealthiest men in the colony.

Harvey was finally able to return to England, probably in 1641. There he found Anthony Panton continuing his campaign of defamation against him. Panton was not content to accuse the previous government in Virginia of every sort of general crime (although he failed to cite any specific instance of oppression) but charged that the commission the King had granted to Sir William Berkeley in August 1641 to replace Wyatt had been surreptitiously obtained. The House of Lords therefore ordered Berkeley's voyage delayed while they examined the case. The House of Commons, on the basis of an earlier petition from

Panton, had similarly prevented the return to Virginia of Richard Kemp, Secretary of the colony, and Christopher Wormeley. Both Berkeley and the two Virginians presented counterpetitions, the one pointing out that he was charged with nothing and hence desired not to be held up on his costly voyage, the others asserting that all Panton's accusations were untrue and similarly requesting permission to leave. The House of Lords thereupon granted these petitions, sending Panton's charges to the Governor and Council of Virginia for a decision.

THE EARLY ADMINISTRATION OF SIR WILLIAM BERKELEY, 1642-1644: AN ERA OF GOOD FEELING

In March 1642 Sir William Berkeley took up his duties in Virginia and began a career which ended both gloriously and ignominiously thirty-five years later. Berkeley came from a distinguished family, was a graduate of Oxford and the Inns of Court, a playwright, and a courtier much admired by the King. Men frequently wondered why he chose to waste his talents in the American wilderness when he might have achieved eminence at Court. The mystery will probably ever remain. In Virginia Berkeley had to work with many of the same Councilors who bedeviled Harvey, but Berkeley was able to get along well with them and with the Assembly and people of Virginia. No Governor of Virginia in the seventeenth century was ever so well or so deservedly loved by the people. Since he ended his long career as Governor amidst a colonial rebellion against his rule in 1676, historians have found it hard to determine whether to bestow praise or blame upon him. Usually he is praised for his early years in the government and condemned for his later years, thus taking on a Dr. Jekyll and Mr. Hyde character. The last word has not yet been written on Governor Berkeley, however, and his character may prove to be more consistent than historians have realized.

Berkeley's first action was to join the Burgesses and Council

29

in a violent denunciation of those who were attempting to reinstitute the old Virginia Company's control over the colony. In a "Declaration against the Company" Berkeley and the Assembly asserted that government under the Company had been intolerable and if introduced again would destroy all the democratic rights allowed by the King's instructions, such as legal trial by jury, the right to petition the King, and yearly Assemblies. The readmission of the Company would also, the declaration asserted, impeach the "freedom of our trade (which is the blood and life of a commonwealth)." The declaration went on to order that anyone who promoted the restoration of the Company's power would, upon due conviction, be held an enemy to the colony and forfeit his whole estate.

Berkeley's next action was to recommend the repeal of the tax of four pounds of tobacco per poll which formerly had been levied for the Governor's use. The Assembly acknowledged this as "a benefit descending unto us and our posterity . . . contributed to us by our present Governor." Berkeley abolished certain other valuable emoluments due him by virtue of his office "wherein," the Assembly declared, "we may not likewise silence the bounty of our present Governor in preferring the public freedom before his particular profit." Finally Berkeley recommended that taxes be proportioned in some measure "according to mens abilities and estates" rather than by the old poll tax system, and the new scheme was, for a brief period, put into effect.

Governor Berkeley not only showed himself selfless in restraining his own opportunities for profit, but fearless in restraining the colonists' itch for land. A few months before his arrival, the Assembly had authorized settlement both on the north side of the York and in the Rappahannock area, if it could be done in great enough force. Opechancanough was to be offered fifty barrels of corn a year for the area between the York and the Piankatank, although the English proposed to take the area whether Opechancanough accepted the offer or not. Twenty-four years had elapsed before English settlement jumped from the James to the York. Now, ten years after the first settlements on the York, Virginians were settling on the next great river to the north, the Rappahannock. By the time Berkeley arrived, some settlers had established themselves in the area, and many more had claimed grants. Indian hostility was great, however, and soon a number of the settlers returned to more secure areas of the country.

Berkeley, working with the the Assembly of March 1643, obtained a law which provided that the Rappahannock River region should remain "unseated," though grants might be tentatively claimed in the area, until the Governor, Council, and Burgesses, that is, the Grand Assembly, should authorize settlement there. The Governor was attempting to regulate the expansion of the colony so that the twin goals of security for the English and justice for the Indians could both be secured. In this he was not entirely successful, since he could only guide, not arbitrarily direct, the representatives of the people. The rich, virgin land of the frontier exerted a continuing attraction to the tobacco planters, and five years later, in 1648, the restrictions on settlement in the Rappahannock region, as well as in the Potomac region, were officially lifted.

Many other important policy decisions were made at the March 1643 meeting of the Grand Assembly. One of these decisions concerned church government. The first act provided for the establishment of church government according to the Anglican form. Virginia was not formed as a protest against the Church of England, as were the Puritan colonies in New England in large measure. Conformity in religious matters was considered a virtue in Virginia. The Assembly, indeed, enacted that nonconformist ministers be compelled to depart the colony, an act which did much to sour Virginia's relations with New England. What was significant about the act, however, was that, with certain exceptions and qualifications, it gave the vestry of every parish power to elect the minister of the parish. Because established landlords

31

and nobles did not exist to build and endow churches as in England, the representatives of the people, in the vestry, had to assume the role of patron, to build the church, and to provide for the support of the minister. In such circumstances it was natural that much of the power that remained in the hierarchy of church, state, and society in England should, in Virginia, pass to the ordinary people and be exercised through their representatives—the vestry and Burgesses. The people, not the King, became the patron of the Church of England in Virginia. Popular responsibility replaced clerical responsibility and added one more phase of life to those controlled directly by the people in the New World. It is significant that Patrick Henry, years before the Revolution, should first have asserted the doctrine of popular responsibility and authority in a case—the celebrated "Parsons' Cause" —involving the people's authority over the church.

An even more significant indication of the shift in power in the government was the provision in one of the acts of the Assembly of 1643 that appeals from the General Court (composed of the Governor and Council, all appointees of the Crown) should be made to the Grand Assembly (composed of the representatives of the people plus the Governor and Council).

Still another demonstration of the *de facto* shift in power from the Crown to the people was the third act of the 1643 Assembly which declared that the Governor and Council "shall not lay any taxes or impositions upon this collonie their lands or comodities otherwise then by the authority of the Grand Assembly to be leavied and imployed as by the Assembly shall be appointed." The first such law had been passed in March 1624 and renewed in February 1632. The process of wresting control of the purse strings from the representatives of the Crown was to be a long-drawn-out process in America, as indeed it was in England. In Virginia the battle was won without a fight either because the Governors were unable to oppose the power of the Burgesses or because they identified their interests with those of the people.

not make such a peace, they were to erect a fort on the Rappahannock River or between it and the York.

The "break" in the war came with the daring capture of
Opechancanough himself by Governor Berkeley. Berkeley, who
frequently led the troops of the colony in the field, was apprised
of the Indian leader's whereabouts, and with characteristic bold-
ness led a troop of men in a raid on his headquarters. The raid
was successful: Opechancanough was captured and brought back
to Jamestown. The old chief, said to be over 100 years, acted
the part of Emperor of the Indian confederation with grave dignity. The historian Robert Beverley tells us that one day the
nearly blind warrior heard "a great noise of the treading of people
about him; upon which he caused his eye-lids to be lifted up;
and finding that a crowd of people were let in to see him, he call'd
in high indignation for the Governour; who being come, Opechancanough scornfully told him, that had it been his fortune to take
Sir William Berkeley prisoner, he should not meanly have ex-
posed him as a show to the people." Berkeley accepted the rebuke,
and ordered him treated with all the dignity due his position as
the leader of many Indian nations. Unfortunately the life of
Opechancanough was shortly after snuffed out by one of his
guards who shot him in the back, despite his defenseless condition.

Peace was concluded with Necotowance, Opechancanough's
successor, by the first act of the October 1646 Assembly. The
treaty is a document of historic importance. Under its provisions
Necotowance acknowledged that he held his kingdom from the
King of England and that his successors might be appointed or
confirmed by the King's Governors. Twenty beaver skins were
to be paid to the Governor yearly "at the going away of the geese"
in acknowledgment of this subjection. Necotowance and his people were given freedom to inhabit and hunt on the north side
of York River without interference from the English, provided
that if the Governor and Council thought fit to permit any English to inhabit the lower reaches of the peninsula, where land

grants had been made before the massacre, Necotowance first should be acquainted therewith. Necotowance in turn surrendered all claim to the land between the falls of the James and the York rivers downward to Chesapeake Bay. Indians were not allowed on this land unless specially designated as messengers to the English. Similarly it was a felony for an Englishmen to repair to the north side of the York River except temporarily under special conditions authorized by the Governor.

The significance of the treaty lies in the fact that the Indians were to be treated as equals, with equal rights to live on the land with the English and to enjoy the rights of human beings. They were no longer considered as vermin to be exterminated whenever the opportunity presented itself. For the first time in Virginia's history, the Indian was considered to have an unquestioned legal right to the land. The setting aside of a reservation for the Indians into which English intrusion was forbidden marked the end of the "perpetual enmity" policy of earlier days. When differences arose, they might still be settled by peace or by war, but the right of either side to exist would not be questioned.

Despite the improvement in the status of the Indian nations occasioned by the treaty of 1646 it proved impossible to preserve their rights in the face of the enormous increase in English population. The fate of the eastern Indians proved identical to the fate of their western brothers in the nineteenth century, when white population increased around the areas set aside for Indian occupancy. But in Virginia the attempt was made to establish a fair settlement, and Governor Berkeley honestly and courageously labored to keep faith with the Indians, even though he lost popularity and eventually his position as a result.

The Assembly of October 1646 also provided for the maintenance of the forts built during the war. This was done by granting the land on which they were built, plus adjoining acres, to individuals who would guarantee to maintain the forts and to keep a certain number of men constantly on the place. By this method the valuable forts of the colony were preserved, yet the people were spared the heavy taxes that would normally have been necessary to maintain them.

The Assembly made further provision that those who had settled along the Potomac in Northumberland should not be allowed to avoid taxes as they had done during the war. The English in this remote area had evidently ignored the act of the February 1645 Assembly which attempted to tax them, and followed instead their own interests, free from any effective control by Virginia's government during the conflict with Opechancanough.

Finally the October Assembly enacted the strictest and most democratic voting law ever made in Virginia. Not only were all freemen (as well as covenanted servants) allowed to vote, but they were fined 100 pounds of tobacco for failing to do so. This act seems to have continued in effect until 1655 when the Assembly prohibited freemen from voting unless they were also householders.

The Administration of Berkeley in 1647-1648: Trade and Expansion

Following the war Virginia returned to its two great peacetime interests—trade and expansion. In the Assembly of April 1647 Berkeley, the Council, and the Burgesses joined in a declaration which reveals the extent to which the colony relied on Dutch traders. It noted that "absolute necessities" had caused earlier Assemblies to invite the Dutch to trade with the inhabitants of Virginia, "which now for some few yeares they have injoyed with such content, comfort and releife that they esteeme the continuance thereof, of noe lesse consequence then as a relative to theire being and subsistence." Rumors had been raised, the declaration went on, that by a recent ordinance of Parliament, all foreigners were prohibited from trading with any of the English plantations "which wee conceive to bee the invention of some

English merchants on purpose to affright and expell the Dutch, and make way for themselves to monopolize not onely our labours and fortunes, but even our persons." The declaration noted the baneful effects on the colony of the greed of the English merchants and pointed out that by ancient charter and right the inhabitants of Virginia were allowed to trade with any nation in amity with the King. It would be inconceivable that Parliament would abridge this right "especially without hearing of the parties principally interested, which infringeth noe lesse the libertye of the Collony and a right of deare esteeme to free borne persons: *viz.*, that no lawe should bee established within the kingdome of England concerninge us without the consent of a grand Assembly here." But since they had heard nothing officially concerning the rumored act, "wee can interprett noe other thing from the report, then a forgerye of avaritious persons, whose sickle hath bin ever long in our harvest allreadye." To provide for Virginia's subsistence the Governor, Council, and Burgesses ordered that the right of the Dutch nation to trade with Virginia be reiterated and preserved, and her traders given every protection.

Virginia's other great problem, that of unregulated expansion, was dealt with by the Grand Assembly of November 1647 in an extraordinary way. The Governor, Council, and Burgesses ordered that persons inhabiting Northumberland and "other remote and straying plantations on the south side of Patomeck River, Wicokomoko, Rappahannock and Fleets Bay" be displanted and removed. They justified this act on the basis of frequent instructions from the King to Berkeley and the Council directing that the planters not be allowed to scatter themselves too widely, and also because they considered such settlement "pernicious" and "destructive" to the peace and safety of the colony, animating the Indians to attack, and thus imbroiling the country in troublesome and expensive wars. Since winter was approaching, the inhabitants were allowed one year to remove themselves to the south side of York River.

The same session of the Assembly authorized Capt. Edward Hill and others to establish, at the head of Rappahannock River, a military and trading outpost which was deemed valuable to the peace and safety of the colony. Hill and his associates were to provide forty men to man the fort which was not to exceed five acres at most, on pain of having the grant revoked.

It was a brave and sensible policy which Berkeley and the Assembly pursued, but one that was destined to be overridden by the power, self-interest, and numbers of the thousands of new members of the colony, both those being born in Virginia in ever-increasing numbers, and those who had left behind them the civil strife of England. In less than a year the Assembly enacted that the tract of land between the Rappahannock and Potomac rivers should be called Northumberland and that it should have power to elect Burgesses. The reasons of "state" that had convinced the Assembly of November 1647 to order the utter dissolution of the Northumberland settlements were thus thrown to the winds by the next Assembly. No doubt the pressure of the inhabitants, would-be inhabitants, and speculators, in addition to the difficulty of enforcing the decision, caused the repeal of the act. The restraining hand of the Governor was never again to be felt as it had been in the period following the 1646 peace. The explosive growth of settlement in Virginia had proved impossible to control.

The justification of the settlement south of the Potomac River was not the only victory of the people in the Assembly of October 1648. Upon the representation of the Burgesses to the Governor and Council complaining of the worn-out lands and insufficient cattle ranges of the earlier settlements, the Governor and Council, after long debate, joined the Burgesses in authorizing settlement on the north side of the York and Rappahannock rivers. The act declared, however, that "for reasons of state to . . . [the Governor and Council] appearing, importing the safety of the people in their seating," no one was to go there before the first of September of the following year. Surveys of the area were allowed at once, however, and land patents were authorized to be taken out. The act making it a felony to go to the north side of York River was repealed. The settlers' and speculators' victory was complete. Reasons of "policy" and "state" proved only of sufficient power to delay the inevitable.

EXECUTION OF CHARLES I AND CAPTURE OF COLONY BY PARLIAMENTARY FORCES, 1649-1652

On January 30, 1649, King Charles I was beheaded by the Parliamentary forces. It was a logical climax to the turmoil into which English institutions and values had been cast by the long years of civil war that preceded the deed. The execution of the King shocked Englishmen as well as foreigners. The reaction of the Virginians came in the form of Act I of the Assembly of October 1649 which hailed "the late most excellent and now undoubtedly sainted king," denounced the perpetrators of the deed, and declared that if any person in the colony should defend "the late traiterous proceedings . . . under any notion of law and justice" by words or speeches, such person should be adjudged an accessory *post factum* to the death of the King. Anyone who expressed doubt, by words and speeches, as to the inherent right of Charles II to succeed his father as King of England and Virginia, was likewise to be adjudged guilty of high treason.

The death of Charles I left the Parliamentary forces supreme in England. Some royalists retired to the continent of Europe, and some came to Virginia. England became a Commonwealth without a King; Oliver Cromwell was later named Protector. The new government, after consolidating its power in England, attempted to extend its control over the colonies, some of which, like Virginia, continued to demonstrate their loyalty to royal authority. On October 3, 1650, Parliament, as a punitive measure, prohibited the trade of the colonies with foreign nations except as the Parliamentary government should allow. "This succession

42

to the exercise of the kingly authority," wrote Jefferson later, "gave the first colour for parliamentary interference with the colonies, and produced that fatal precedent which they continued to follow after they had retired, in other respects, within their proper functions."

The reaction of the Virginia Burgesses to this act was as violent as their reaction to the beheading of Charles I. Their temper on both occasions owed much to the eloquence of their Governor, and to the admiration in which he was held by the people. In March 1651 they met to consider the Parliamentary threat to their beliefs and to their livelihood. Sir William Berkeley spoke to them on the subject of Parliament's claim to speak for the English nation. Said the Governor:

If the whole current of their reasoning were not as ridiculous, as their actions have been tyrannicall and bloudy, we might wonder with what browes they could sustaine such impertinent assertions: For if you looke into it, the strength of their argument runs onely thus: we have laid violent hands on your land-lord, possessed his manner house where you used to pay your rents, therfore now tender your respects to the same house you once reverenced. . . . They talke indeed of money laid out on this country in its infancy: I will not say how little, nor how centuply repaid, but will onely aske, was it theirs? . . . Surely Gentlemen we are more slaves by nature, then their power can make us if we suffer our selves to be shaken with these paper bulletts, and those on my life are the heaviest they either can or will send us.

Berkeley was confident that if Virginia put up a determined resistance, the new English rulers would beg the colony to trade with them. He compared the state of England with the state of Virginia, to the disadvantage of the former. The Parliamentary government of England, he asserted, did not represent the will of the people who would not endure their "slavery, if the sword at their throats did not compell them to languish under the misery they howrely suffer." As for Virginia, "there is not here an arbitrary hand that dares to touch the substance of either poore or rich." Berkeley called on the Burgesses to support his stand against the act, asking:

What is it can be hoped for in a change, which we have not allready? Is it liberty? The sun looks not on a people more free then we are from all oppression. Is it wealth? Hundreds of examples shew us that industry and thrift in a short time may bring us to as high a degree of it, as the country and our conditions are yet capable of: Is it securety to enjoy this wealth when gotten? With out blushing I will speake it, I am confident theare lives not that person can accuse me of attempting the least act against any mans property. Is it peace? The Indians, God be blessed round about us are subdued; we can onely feare the Londoners, who would faine bring us to the same poverty, wherein the Dutch found and relieved us; would take away the liberty of our consciences, and tongues, and our right of giving and selling our goods to whom we please. But Gentlemen by the Grace of God we will not so tamely part with our King, and all these blessings we enjoy under him; and if they oppose us, do but follow me, I will either lead you to victory, or loose a life which I cannot more gloriously sacrifice then for my loyalty, and your security.

The speech being ended the House of Burgessses, unanimously with the Governor and Council, agreed to reject the Parliamentary act of October 3, 1650, as illegal, and to continue in allegiance to King Charles II, always praying for his restoration to the throne and for the repentance of those who, "to the hazard of their soules" opposed him. The Assembly proclaimed that they would continue to trade freely with all persons of whatever nation who came to trade with them, not excluding the Londoners.

This assertion of Virginia's traditional freedom and rights was, of course, a direct challenge to the Parliamentary government. In the fall of 1651 that government determined to chastise the rebellious colony and subject it by force. A fleet was dispatched in October to conquer Virginia and Barbados, another rebellious colony. Robert Dennis, Richard Bennett, Thomas Stegge, and William Claiborne were chosen commissioners to take over the government of Virginia once it had been conquered. Bennett and Claiborne were living in Virginia at the time.

Part of the fleet arrived in Virginia waters in January 1652. Berkeley called upon the people to prepare for resistance. One thousand troops, it is said, gathered in James City for the purpose. Five hundred Indian allies of the colony promised their aid. Berkeley denounced the leaders of the Parliamentary expedition as bloody tyrants, pirates, and robbers. He warned the Virginians that, if they did not repel the attack, their land titles would be thrown into doubt and they would be brought under a company of merchants who would order them at their pleasure and keep them from trade with all others. To counteract the Governor's influence, the Parliamentary commissioners circulated letters and declarations throughout the country denying any such evil intentions. Finally, on January 19, they sent a summons to the Governor and Council to surrender, and set sail from the lower reaches of the James to Jamestown. A milder answer than expected was returned, setting forth various demands and privileges desired by the Virginians.

The commissioners' reply to these proposals was favorable enough to cause Berkeley to call an Assembly, and negotiations were entered into between the Governor, Council, and Burgesses on the one hand, and the Parliamentary commissioners on the other. Articles of submission were agreed upon which were honorable to both sides, Virginia receiving guarantees of the privileges of freeborn people of England, authority for the Grand Assembly to continue to function, guarantees of immunity for acts or words done or spoken in opposition to Parliament, guarantees of the bounds of Virginia, of the fifty-acre headright privilege, and of the right to "free trade as the people of England do enjoy to all places and with all nations according to the lawes of that commonwealth." Special provisions were made which allowed the Governor and Council to refrain from taking any oath to the Commonwealth for one year and guaranteed them for one year from censure for speaking well of the King in their private houses. Berkeley and the Council were given leave to sell their estates and quit Virginia, either for England or Holland. No penalties were to be imposed on those who had served the King.

The commissioners of Parliament considered that they had been lucky to reduce the colony without bloodshed, even though forced to agree to such mild terms. At the same time the event suggests that the bitterness which existed in England between Roundheads and Cavaliers was not quite so extreme in the colonies, where little blood had been shed for the cause of either. The colonies had interests of their own which ran counter to those of the mother country, whether in the hands of King or Parliament. Governor, Council, and Burgesses in Virginia were closer to each other economically and politically than they were to their respective counterparts in England. What held the colonies to the mother country was not self-interest but ties of historical tradition and racial patriotism. The execution of Charles I and seizure of the colony by the Parliamentary fleet loosened these ties. The Crown, symbol of continuity with past ages of English subjects and of unity among all the King's realms, was now not only removed but denounced by those who had done the deed.

Virginia never showed sympathy for those who had killed the King, and the Assembly took to heart Governor Berkeley's warning of 1651 that the blood of Charles I "will yet staine your garments if you willingly submit to those murtherers hands that shed it." It is true that following the surrender the Parliamentary commissioners agreed with the representatives of the people on a provisional government for Virginia, but the bonds that held Virginia to England had lost much of the cement of love and tradition. Local and self-interest were now to dominate to a great extent Virginia's actions. Such motives had always been latent, and indeed active. But under royal government, the Governor could often exert a countervailing force to prevent such interests from overriding the interests of nation and morality.

Under the terms of the settlement the Grand Assembly was to continue to function, and the Assembly and commissioners agreed that Richard Bennett, one of the commissioners, should act as Governor for a year. It was expected that orders would shortly arrive from England establishing new patterns of government. Such instructions were especially necessary to determine the role and authority of the Governor and Council, formerly appointed by the King. The new rulers in England were made aware of the need for a new policy for the colonies, but they never found time to make the necessary decisions. At intervals the colonists were informed that Cromwell had not forgotten them and that His Highness would soon let them know his pleasure. But instructions never came except spasmodically and inadequately. The merchants who stood to gain from the Navigation Act of 1651, which generally excluded foreign ships from the colonies and attempted to restrain colonial trade with foreign countries, complained at the failure of the colonists to obey the act and demanded that orders be sent to enforce it, but no adequate provisions were ever made.

Thus the colony was left to its own devices during the period. Virginia traders paid little attention to Parliamentary restrictions on their commerce. They insisted that the provision of the Articles of Surrender allowing them free trade with all nations according to the laws of the Commonwealth did not prevent them from trading with foreigners. They argued that since the first article of the surrender agreement guaranteed them the rights of freeborn Englishmen, an act discriminating against them in matters of trade because they happened to live in the colonies was illegal. Dutch ships called often, though perhaps not so frequently as some have believed, and individual Virginians traded as they pleased with the Dutch and English colonies in America.

EXPANSION IN VIRGINIA, 1650-1656

The existence of a weak executive, dependent on the people for his authority, inevitably brought about a dispersal of power and authority from the center to the outer edges of settlement.

The explosive force of expansion was no longer limited by the strong hand of a royal Governor, and each increment of population in the colony and power in the hands of the local authorities added fuel to the combustion.

One of Virginia's frontiers at this time was the Eastern Shore. It was a frontier community because the law of the colonial government in Jamestown rarely extended to it. The local commissioners of the county court, later called "justices," provided what justice existed on the Eastern Shore. But since these commissioners were sometimes the worst offenders against the policies of the Governor, Council, and Burgesses, justice was often sacrificed to interest, especially when Indians were involved. The leaders on the Eastern Shore, like Edmund Scarborough, were among the richest men and greatest landowners of the colony. They conducted the county's business as if it were their own, which indeed it was to a great extent. Their oppression of the Eastern Shore Indians makes a sorry history, despite the efforts of Governor Berkeley to restrain them. In April 1650, for example, Berkeley was forced to write to the commissioners of Northampton asking them not to allow any land to be taken from the Laughing King Indians. Berkeley pointed out that during the massacre of 1644 these Indians had remained faithful to the English. How could Virginia expect them to do the same again, asked Berkeley, "unless we correspond with them in acts of charity and amity, especially unless we abstain from acts of rapine and violence, which they say we begin to do, by taking away their land from them, by pretence of the sale of a patent."

Honest attempts were made both before and after the retirement of Sir William Berkeley in 1652 to restrain the frontier barons in their savage attacks on unsuspecting Indian towns. But often the law was too weak and the guilty too strong. Neither the Indians in front of them nor the government behind them had the power to curb their desires except in a limited fashion. This was one of the benefits—to the frontiersmen—of living under English law. The government could not effectively restrain the Englishman nor protect the Indian. As a result the reckless expansion went on into the lands of other tribes. As each new Indian tribe was reached the same dismal pattern of subjugation or extirpation was repeated, despite the efforts of the Governor and Council to see that the rights of the Indians were preserved.

Every extension of settlement strengthened local rule. In May 1652 the people of Northampton County, which comprised the whole of the Eastern Shore of Virginia, protested to the Assembly against a tax levied on them, asserting that since they had not sent representatives to the Assembly since 1647, except for one Burgess in 1651, they did not think the Assembly could tax them. They asked that they be allowed to have a separate government and the right to try all causes in their own courts. Although Northampton was not allowed to dissociate itself entirely from the rest of Virginia, acts of 1654 and 1656 allowed the county to constitute laws and customs for itself on matters dealing with Indians and manufactures.

Virginia's most important frontier region in the 1650's was the area along the Potomac River, although settlement went on simultaneously westward up the James, York, and Rappahannock, southward into Carolina, and northward up the Eastern Shore to Maryland. Sometimes individuals obtained grants to explore, settle, and monopolize the trade of these regions. But usually the expansion was catch as catch can. Since land travel was still more difficult than water travel, expansion up the Potomac, the last great unsettled tidewater river, was fastest. Individuals who already had plantations in the older areas of settlement around Jamestown sailed their barques up the Potomac and, without bothering to go ashore, took the bounds of likely pieces of land. The best spots were often the corn fields of the Indians and sometimes the very towns where they lived. The fact that the Indians occupied the land counted for little in the thoughts of the settlers and speculators who flocked to the area.

Following their surveys, the explorers rushed back to James City and put in claims for the waterfront acreages, presenting one "headright"—proof that someone had been imported into the colony by their agency—for every fifty acres. The Patent Books of the colony frequently show signs of fraud in the presentation of headrights. Occasionally more land was granted than the claimant was entitled to on the basis of the headrights he presented. But the headright system, even imperfectly administered, remained during the Parliamentary period as one of the elements of restraint on the unbounded desires of the planters. Land acquisition was thus tied in a fixed ratio to population increase. There was, as a result, some assurance that land acquired would be populated and farmed. It was not until late in the seventeenth century that anyone could buy land for money alone, a practice which enabled some individuals in the eighteenth century to obtain holdings exceeding 100,000 acres. In the middle of the seventeenth century 10,000 acres was a practical "top" limit.

At the beginning of the Commonwealth period in Virginia a number of new counties were set up. The Assembly of April 1652 listed two new ones: Gloucester, north of the York, and Lancaster, north of the Rappahannock. The Assembly of November 1652 listed Surry, south of the James, for the first time. Settlers had moved into these areas earlier when they were parts of other counties, and in two cases the county organization may have been set up prior to April 1652. The Assembly of July 1653, in addition to authorizing exploration and settlement on the Roanoke and Chowan rivers in present-day North Carolina, and exploration into the Appalachian Mountains, ordered that a county to be called Westmoreland should be set up west of Northumberland County on the Potomac, with boundaries from Machodoc River to the falls of the Potomac above the town of the Anacostan Indians. It was thus intended not only to include in the new county all the lands of the Doeg Indians, but also those of the Anacostans. The Assembly of November 1654 authorized the establishment of New Kent County along both sides of the upper York River and far up the Pamunkey and Mattaponi rivers.

The Assembly of November 1654 also authorized the three new northern counties of Lancaster, Northumberland, and Westmoreland to march against the Rappahannock Indians to punish various "injuries and insolencies offered" by them. One hundred men were to be raised in Lancaster, forty in Northumberland, and thirty in Westmoreland. The commissioners of these counties were authorized to raise the troops, and one of their number was appointed commander-in-chief of the expedition. He was to march to the Rappahannock Indian town and demand and receive "such satisfaction as he shall thinke fitt for the severall injuries done unto the said inhabitants not using any acts of hostility but defensive in case of assault." The charge of the war was to be borne by the three counties concerned. This expedition was like many others that both preceded and followed it. In each case, enormous authority and responsibility were given to local officials who were themselves frequently the leading oppressors of the Indians. Such expeditions not infrequently took on the character of private wars between the big landowners of the frontier and the Indian towns in the vicinity. The Governor, Council, and Burgesses frequently heard the complaints of the local settlers, but rarely the complaints of the Indians. The authorization to the local community to administer justice to the Indians often proved a cover for their expulsion or extirpation.

The usual grievances of the settlers against the Indians were not the violent murders and massacres so often associated in the public mind with Indian-white relations, but minor irritations concerning property and animals. The settlers let their hogs run wild. The hogs would get into the Indians' corn. The Indians would kill the hogs. The settlers would demand satisfaction. Many acts of the Assembly testify to the fact that shooting of wild hogs was one of the most frequent points of dispute not only between the English and the Indians but among the English themselves.

It was one reason why early Assemblies provided strict rules for erecting adequate fences around cultivated fields and establishing lines of responsibility for damage caused by straying cattle or hogs. On the frontier, however, such refinements of civilization as fences were long in coming. What was more natural than that the same conflicts which arose among the English in the early years of settlement should arise between the English and the Indians on the frontier. The tragedy was that English-Indian conflicts were not normally settled in the courts as were conflicts between Englishmen. The courts did deal with Indian-white conflicts to a certain extent, but, as noted before, the local justices were often the very persons the Indians accused of oppressing them. Sometimes the Indians were able to bring their complaints before the General Court in Jamestown. But often the dispute was settled in the wilderness in the traditional frontier way: by violence. Since the settlers had weapons of violence superior to those possessed by the Indians, it was not very frequently that the Indians won their "case."

In the Assemblies of these years there is occasional mention of the splitting of counties in two parts, or of the formation of new parishes. Usually these divisions were made along rivers or streams. Such legislation suggests that settlement was spreading back from the water routes into the land area between streams. The early counties were normally set up to embrace the area on both sides of watercourses, even broad rivers like the James and York. The rivers were, in the early period of settlement, bonds that linked the settlers on either side to each other. It was natural that rivers should be the principal thoroughfares of the country. But as settlement spread into the interior, up the tributary streams that issued into the larger rivers, the natural social unit that developed was that of communities on the same side of the river. Hence the gradual conversion of rivers into political boundaries.

The Assembly of March 1655, for the first time in Virginia's history, restricted the voting privilege to "housekeepers whether freeholders, leaseholders, or otherwise tenants." Freemen who could not qualify as householders, even though they may have been grown sons living in their father's house, could not vote. It is significant that this first restriction on the right to vote in Virginia came not under a royal governor, but under so-called "Parliamentary" rule. So unpopular was this enactment that it was amended by an act of the Assembly of March 1656 on the grounds that "we conceive it something hard and unagreeable to reason that any persons shall pay equall taxes and yet have no votes in elections." Freemen were again allowed to vote provided that they did not do so "in a tumultuous way."

The Assembly of March 1656 passed an act which attempted to solve the Indian problem in a way that had never been tried before but has been frequently tried since. The plan was to encourage the growth of an acquisitive spirit among the Indians to serve as a counterweight to the acquisitive spirit of the English. The preamble to the act asserted that the danger of war from the Indians stemmed from two causes: "our extreame pressures on them and theire wanting of something to hazard and loose beside their lives." Therefore the Assembly enacted that for every eight wolves' heads brought in by the Indians, the King or great man of the Indians should have a cow delivered to him at the public charge. "This will be a step to civilizing them and to making them Christians," the act went on; "besides it will certainly make the comanding Indians watch over their own men that they do us no injuries, knowing that by theire default they may be in danger of losing their estates." The Assembly also attempted to make the lands possessed by the Indians under the seal of the colony inalienable to the English. Otherwise, constant pressure on the Indians by the settlers would force them over and over again to dispose of their lands.

Many people fail to realize that the Indians of Virginia lived in well-defined towns or settlements. It was, indeed, the Indians who lived an "urban" life in the seventeenth century while the English settlers were usually scattered about the countryside. The conventional picture of the Indian roaming the forests, living solely by hunting and fishing, is mistaken. The Indian did hunt and fish, as many of us do today. But his support came in large measure from the corn and vegetables growing in the fields which adjoined every Indian town. The Indians had a close-knit and harmonious community life. They were only indirectly touched by the white man's money economy and were usually content to raise only what food they needed for their own consumption. They were not infected with the restless, individualistic spirit of the white settler who constantly worked to accumulate a monetary surplus from the returns on his single cash crop, tobacco.

Like later attempts to destroy the group-centered society of the Indians in favor of a self-centered society, this attempt of 1656 was not completely successful.

Indian Troubles, 1656-1658

Early in 1656 word was received that six or seven hundred strange Indians from the mountains had come down and seated themselves near the falls of the James. The March Assembly, considering how much blood it had cost to "expell and extirpate those perfidious and treacherous Indians which were there formerly," and considering how the area lay within the limits "which in a just warr were formerly conquered by us," ordered the two upper counties under Col. Edward Hill to send 100 men to remove the intruders peacefully, making war only in self-defense. Messages were sent to obtain the aid of the Pamunkeys, Chickahominies, and other neighboring Indians. Tottopottomoy, the King of the Pamunkeys, joined Hill with 100 of his warriers, although only the summer before his brother had been murdered by an Englishman.

The western Indians had apparently come down to treat with the English about trade, bringing with them many beaver skins to begin the commerce. Col. Hill, however, despite the Assembly's command to avoid the use of force, perfidiously had five of the kings who came to parley with him put to death. "This unparalleled hellish treachery and anti-christian perfidy more to be detested than any heathenish inhumanity," a contemporary wrote, "cannot but stink most abominably in the nosetrils of as many Indians, as shall be infested with the least scent of it, even to their perpetual abhorring and abandoning of the very sight and name of an English man, till some new generation of a better extract shall be transplanted among them!" In the fight that ensued Tottopottomoy lost his life fighting bravely for the English. Despite his fidelity, neither he nor his tribe was honorably treated by the English, the very land he owned being extorted from him and his successors.

Hill himself was found guilty by the unanimous vote of the Burgesses and Council of "crimes and weaknesses" in his conduct of the campaign. He was ordered suspended from all offices, military and civil, and made liable for the charge of procuring a peace with the Indians with whom he had so treacherously dealt.

The disgraceful episode of Hill's campaign may have caused some soul-searching in the Assembly that met following the event, for, in addition to censuring Hill, it repealed an act which had made it lawful to kill an Indian committing a trespass. It pointed out that since the oath of the person killing the Indian was considered sufficient evidence to prove the alleged trespass, killing Indians, "though never so innocent," had come to be of "small account" with the settlers. Since the colony would probably be involved in endless wars and might "expect a success answerable to the injustice of our beginning if no act be made for the future to prevent this wanton and unnecessary shedding of blood," the Assembly attempted to provide some protection for the Indians.

That expansion into the Indians' territory continued is shown by the authorization given by this same Assembly of December 1656 to form the county of Rappahannock on both sides of the Rappahannock River above Lancaster County. Confirmation of the movement towards the frontier is shown in the report to the same Assembly by the sheriffs of Isle of Wight County and Elizabeth City County, both at the mouth of the James River, that their counties were overrated in the tax lists of "tithable" persons by thirty-eight and thirty-two persons respectively. The Assembly ordered that their tax allotments should be reduced accordingly and laid upon Lancaster County "where they are increased since the last year's list 152 persons." An act of the Assembly of March 1658 similarly took note of the numbers of inhabitants who had "deserted their plantations and receded into the bay of Chisapeake" without having satisfied their creditors. It prescribed penalties for removing without notice.

Bills guaranteeing the Indians their lands, justice, and personal freedom continued to pass. The acts freely admitted that previous guarantees to this effect had been ineffective and that "manie English doe still intrench upon the said Indians' land," which the Assembly conceived to be "contrary to justice, and the true intent of the English plantation in this country." Nevertheless attempts to legislate justice for the Indians continued. It could not be done. The power of the Assembly's acts was not equal to the power of the frontiersmen's muskets. However, the acts of the Assembly were not without effect, and in many cases served their purpose. One of the most notable acts of this Assembly provided that no grants of land should be made to any Englishman in the future until the Indians had first been guaranteed fifty acres for each bowman. The good intent of this act seems to have been a direct consequence of the practice that had arisen in the preceding years of granting patents to Englishmen for land occupied by the Indians. It was an attempt to make sure that the Indians would not be wholly dispossessed to satisfy the land hunger of the English.

OLIVER CROMWELL
Painting by Robert Walker

Early writers on Virginia history tended to overemphasize how completely affairs in Virginia during the Commonwealth and Protectorate periods were in the hands of the House of Burgesses. Still, the House did assume to itself many of the powers of government in the period and asserted its ultimate authority in all other matters. It took this position out of necessity, and always with the proviso that, should instructions come from the supreme power in England, it would obey them.

The first Governor under the Commonwealth, Richard Bennett, was appointed by an act of Assembly on April 30, 1652, his term to last for one year or until the following meeting of the Assembly, with the further proviso that the appointment should be in effect "untill the further pleasures of the states be knowne." Bennett, a planter of Nansemond County, was a Puritan in his religious outlook and was one of those who had invited New England to send ministers to Virginia in the early 1640's. When Parliament decided to conquer the colony in 1651 it appointed him one of the commissioners for the enterprise. It is probable that the secret instructions issued to Bennett by the Parliamentary authorities required him to come to some agreement with the Burgesses on who should be Governor until a more formal commission for the office should issue from the supreme power in England. However, as the years passed, and as instructions from England failed to deal with Virginia's problems, the House of Burgesses asserted its prerogative more and more.

On March 31, 1655, Edward Digges was elected Governor by the Assembly to replace Bennett. Digges was the son of Sir Dudley Digges, Master of the Rolls under Charles I. He came to Virginia sometime before 1650 and bought a plantation on the York River, subsequently known as "Bellfield." The plantation become famous for the quality of the tobacco grown there, and was also the scene of Digges's efforts at silk production, in the culture of which he employed three Armenians. When Digges decided to return to England in 1656, Samuel Mathews was elected to succeed him. There is some confusion as to whether Governor Mathews was the man who so bedeviled Sir John Harvey in the 1630's, or his son of the same name.

When Mathews and the Council attempted to dissolve the Assembly on April 1, 1658, the Burgesses answered that the Governor's action was illegal, and that they would remain and complete their work. Mathews refused to concede their point formally, though he declared his willingness to allow them to continue in fact while the dispute was submitted to the Lord Protector in England. The Burgesses declared his answer unsatisfactory. They demanded a specific acknowledgment that the House remained undissolved. Mathews and the Council finally agreed to revoke the declaration of dissolution, but still insisted on referring the dispute to the Lord Protector. The House rejected this answer as well, asserting that the present power of Virginia resided in the Burgesses, who were not dissolvable by any power extant in Virginia but themselves. They directed the High Sheriff of James City County not to execute any warrant but from the Speaker of the House. In addition, they ordered Col. William Claiborne, the Secretary of the Council, to surrender the records of the country into the hands of John Smith, the Speaker of the Assembly, on the basis of the Burgesses' declaration to hold "supreame power of this country."

That the House of Burgesses did not mean its actions to be in defiance of the power that existed in England, however, is shown by its agreement to proclaim Richard, son of Oliver Cromwell, Lord Protector when the Governor sent down, at the March 1659 session, an official letter from His Highness' Council requiring that it be done. Immediately after agreeing to proclaim Richard, the Burgesses decided to address the new Lord Protector for confirmation of the privilege granted to the Assembly, perhaps under the terms of Bennett's secret instructions, to elect its own officers. Although the Speaker of the House assured the Burgesses that the Governor was willing to join them in such a request, some of the Burgesses expressed a desire to hear the assurance from the Governor's own lips. Accordingly, he was sent for and, to the satisfaction of the Burgesses, "acknowledged the supream power of electing officers to be by the present lawes resident in the Grand Assembly." He promised to join them in requesting confirmation of these privileges from His Highness.

The Assembly, at this same session, passed an act electing Mathews Governor again for two years "and then the Grand Assembly to elect a Governour as they shall think fitt." The act was to be in force "until his Highness pleasure be further signified." William Claiborne was appointed Secretary of State on his acknowledgment that he received the place from the Assembly, and with the proviso that he should continue Secretary until the next Assembly or until the Lord Protector's pleasure should be further signified to the colony.

The Assembly of 1659 marks the high water point of local government in Virginia. Not only were the Burgesses supreme in matters of general legislation, compelling the Governor and Secretary to bow to their sovereign power, but in their home counties affairs were conducted much as the local justices saw fit. The Assembly of 1659 even authorized free trade with the Indians by anyone in any goods—even guns and ammunition. Never before had regulation on a point of such vital interest to the security of the colony been so utterly abandoned.

RECALL OF SIR WILLIAM BERKELEY BY THE ASSEMBLY, 1659-1660

Soon after the Assembly of March 1659 ended, Richard Cromwell resigned the reins of government in England. The English nation was again plunged into turmoil. Letters arriving in Virginia spoke of the people divided "some for one Government some for another." The prospect of London "burned into Ashes and the streets running with blood" was held a likely outcome of the divisions.

In the midst of this troublous situation, Governor Mathews died. The next Assembly met in March 1660. In a move that has astonished historians since that time it asked Sir William Berkeley, the royal Governor whom its former leaders had deposed, to govern Virginia again. No royal banners were unfurled; Charles II was not proclaimed King. The House of Burgesses, holding the supreme power in the colony, merely offered the governorship to the man who had been universally admired for his justice, humanity, and willingness to sacrifice his own interest to that of the colony.

Berkeley had been unwilling to disavow his loyalty to the Crown in 1652 and he was not prepared to do so now. He replied to the Burgesses' invitation by saying that he would not dare to offend the King by accepting a commission to govern from any power in England opposed to him. He urged them to choose instead a more vigorous man from amongst their own number. But he did offer to accept the governorship directly from the House of Burgesses if the Council would concur with the Burgesses in offering it to him. He promised that if thereafter any supreme power in England succeeded in re-establishing its authority in Virginia he would immediately lay down his commission and "will live most submissively obedient to any power God shall set over me, as the experience of eight yeares have shewed I have done." He would not refuse their call, he wrote, if they accepted his conditions, for "I should be worthily thought hospitall mad, if I would not change povertie for wealth,—contempt for honor."

The Council on March 21, 1660, unanimously concurred in the Burgesses' choice of Berkeley as Governor, and the King's loyal servant was thereupon installed in the office.

Some historians have seen the election of Berkeley as the signal for a royalist purge of the Parliamentary influences that

60

were thought to have existed in the colony since 1652. A study of the membership of the House of Burgesses, Council, and county courts, however, shows a continuity of membership which extends from before the Parliamentary seizure of the colony until after the restoration of King Charles II. The evidence suggests that there was no violent division between royalists and Parliamentarians in Virginia. The people were Virginians first and royalists or Parliamentarians second. The solidarity of their political interests was a harbinger of the American independence that was slowly to mature in the next century.

On May 29, 1660, the birthday of Charles II, that monarch returned to London and was restored to the throne of England. Word of the restoration was received in Virginia in the fall, and Berkeley ordered the sheriffs and chief officers of all counties to proclaim Charles II King of England, and to cause all writs and warrants from that time on to issue in His Majesty's name. The Assembly of March 1661, taking into consideration the fact that the colony, by submitting to the "execrable power" of the Parliamentary forces, had thereby become guilty of the crimes of that power, enacted that January 30, the day Charles I was beheaded, should "be annually solemnized with fasting and prayers that our sorrowes may expiate our crime and our teares wash away our guilt." Another act declared May 29, the day of Charles II's birth and restoration, a holy day to be annually celebrated "in testimony of our thankfulnesse and joy."

Thus ended the brief period in which Virginia's government was turned upside down and permanent alteration caused in her relations with England. Although the King once more became the symbol of the unity of the colony and the mother country, the royal prerogative would never again be blindly accepted by the people of either place. Larger developments in the economic, social, and intellectual spheres were bringing to an end the era of all-powerful Kings. Power had descended to the lower ranks of society, and that power was beginning to be brought into play.

This larger shift of power has been chronicled in the story of Virginia from 1625 to 1660. It is the story of a small community of Englishmen transplanted to American shores, living for a time subject to traditional English restraints, then, in a period of rapid expansion, losing their cohesiveness and their values under the impact of the American experience and their own natures. Their political expression soon passed from a passive to an active mode. The law became something they made, not something someone else applied to them. Land was similarly not something bestowed on them by generous parents, but something one took from Nature, or Nature's surrogate, the Indian. Labor was no longer a privilege allowed the individual by the community, but a precious gift contributed by the individual to the community. In sum, the ordinary people who had removed themselves to the New World soon discovered that they were no longer humble servants of great lords, but were themselves lords of the American earth. If they had the power why not exercise it? The process by which the rulers of the people were forced to become the "servants" of their "subjects" thereupon began. The culmination of this rearrangement of the political atoms of society was the War for Independence of 1776. Whether the swing from authority to liberty was for good or for evil is not for the historian to say.

BIBLIOGRAPHY

Another booklet in this series contains a selected bibliography of works on seventeenth-century Virginia. The interested student should consult that booklet for a more detailed listing of works used in preparing this account of Virginia in the period 1625-1660.

The best secondary account of Virginia in the period covered by this booklet is Wesley Frank Craven, *The Southern Colonies in the Seventeenth Century, 1607-1689* (Baton Rouge, 1949). Craven skilfully combines research in Virginia local history with a broad understanding of developments in England and in other colonies. He points out the social and political significance of many hitherto ignored aspects of Virginia history. Other important works include Charles McLean Andrews, *The Colonial Period of American History,* I (New Haven, 1934), Thomas Jefferson Wertenbaker, *Virginia under the Stuarts* (Princeton, 1914), Herbert L. Osgood, *The American Colonies in the Seventeenth Century,* 3 vols. (New York, 1904-1907), and Edward D. Neill, *Virginia Carolorum: The Colony under the Rule of Charles the First and Second, A.D. 1625-A.D. 1685* (Albany, 1886).

Any study of colonial Virginia must begin with a perusal of Philip Alexander Bruce, *Economic History of Virginia in the Seventeenth Century,* 2 vols. (New York, 1895), and his *Institutional History of Virginia in the Seventeenth Century,* 2 vols. (New York, 1910). Bruce's work is the indispensable platform upon which political and social accounts of the period must rest. Morgan Poitiaux Robinson, *Virginia Counties: Those Resulting from Virginia Legislation* [Virginia State Library, *Bulletin,* IX, Nos. 1-3] (Richmond, 1916), is a carefully documented study of the growth of Virginia as evidenced by the formation of its counties. Maps showing the area of settlement at frequent intervals give a graphic account of the nature and extent of Virginia's expansion.

There are a number of local histories chronicling the growth of particular regions in Virginia. An outstanding local history is Fairfax Harrison, *Landmarks of Old Prince William* (Richmond, 1924), which analyzes the growth of settlement in the Potomac River valley. Histories of the Eastern Shore are numerous: Susie M. Ames, *Studies of the Virginia Eastern Shore in the Seventeenth Century* (Richmond, 1940), Jennings Cropper Wise, *Ye Kingdome of Accawmacke, or the Eastern Shore of Virginia in the Seventeenth Century* (Richmond, 1911), and Ralph T. Whitelaw, *Virginia's Eastern Shore,* 2 vols. (Richmond, 1951).

A reading of but a few works in Virginia history will be enough to show that the interpretations and conclusions of the authors must be accepted with extreme caution. There are two conflicting interpretations

63

for nearly every important event in Virginia's history. History may be defined as the attempt to state what happened in the past on the basis of inadequate evidence existing in the present. The reader should keep always in mind that historical writing is largely a series of guesses more or less intelligently elaborated.

Much of the original manuscript material upon which an account of the period must be based has been published in the following sources: William Waller Hening, *The Statutes at Large; being a Collection of all the Laws of Virginia,* Vol. I (Richmond, 1809), H. R. McIlwaine, *Minutes of the Council and General Court of Colonial Virginia, 1622-1632, 1670-1676* (Richmond, 1924), H. R. McIlwaine, *Journals of the House of Burgesses of Virginia, 1619-1658/59* (Richmond, 1914), Nell Marion Nugent, *Cavaliers and Pioneers: Abstracts of Virginia Land Patents and Grants, 1623-1666* (Richmond, 1934), *Virginia Magazine of History and Biography* (Richmond, 1893 to present), *William and Mary Quarterly* (Williamsburg, 1892 to present), *The Southern Literary Messenger,* January 1845 (documents on the recall of Governor Berkeley by the Burgesses and Council of Virginia in 1660), and W. Noel Sainsbury, *Calendar of State Papers, Colonial Series, 1574-1660, Preserved in the State Paper Department of Her Majesty's Public Record Office* (London, 1860). The essential guide to most of this material is Earl G. Swem, *Virginia Historical Index,* 2 vols. (Roanoke, 1934).

The most important unpublished manuscript materials of the period are the county records, some of which are complete from the earliest period of settlement. Originals or transcripts of the county records are available in the Virginia State Library, Richmond. Another important source of unpublished manuscript material for the period is the "Virginia, Book No. 43" manuscript in the Library of Congress, Washington, D. C., which contains numerous commissions and proclamations for the period 1626-1634. Among the Virginia papers of the Barons of Sackville, Knole Park, are a few documents relating to the period which have not been printed either in the documentary articles in the *American Historical Review,* XXVII (1922), Nos. 3-4, or elsewhere. They are now available on microfilm in the Library of Congress, having been photographed by the British Manuscripts Project of the American Council of Learned Societies.

Important unpublished dissertations include James Kimbrough Owen, "The Virginia Vestry: A Study in the Decline of a Ruling Class" (Ph.D. dissertation, Princeton University, 1947), and Edna Jensen, "Sir John Harvey: Governor of Virginia" (M.A. thesis, University of Virginia, 1950).